Z z

Zlata, Me, and the Letter Z

Alphabet Friends

by Cynthia Klingel and Robert B. Noyed

The
Child's World

The Child's World

Published in the United States of America
by The Child's World®
P.O. Box 326
Chanhassen, MN 55317-0326
800-599-READ
www.childsworld.com

The Child's World®: Mary Berendes, Publishing Director

Editorial Directions, Inc.: E. Russell Primm, Editorial
Director; Emily Dolbear, Line Editor; Ruth Martin,
Editorial Assistant; Linda S. Koutris, Photo Researcher
and Selector

Photographs ©: Nancy R. Cohen/Photodisc/Getty
Images: Cover & 9, 21; Corbis : 10, 17, 18; C Squared
Studios/Photodisc/Getty Images. 13, Photodisc/Getty
Images: 14.

Library of Congress Cataloging-in-Publication Data
Klingel, Cynthia Fitterer.
  Zlata, me, and the letter Z / by Cynthia Klingel and
Robert B. Noyed.
      p. cm. — (Alphabet readers)
Summary: A simple story about two friends and the fun
they have together introduces the letter "z".
  ISBN 1-59296-116-9 (Library Bound : alk. paper)
  [1. Friendship—Fiction. 2. Alphabet.] I. Noyed, Robert
B., ill. II. Title. III. Series.
  PZ7.K6798Zl 2003
  [E]—dc21
                                              2003006617

Note to parents and educators:

The first skill children acquire before becoming successful readers is individual letter recognition. The Alphabet Friends series has been created with the needs of young learners in mind. Each engaging book begins by showing the difference between the capital letter and the lowercase letter. In each of the books on the vowels and the consonants c and g, children are introduced to the different sounds that the letter can make. Finally, children see that the letters can be found at the beginning of a word, in the middle of a word, and in most cases, at the end of a word.

Following the introduction, children meet their Alphabet Friends. The friend in each story encounters many words that include the featured letter of that book. Each noun that begins with the title letter is highlighted in red with the initial letter of the word in bold. Above the word is a rebus drawing that establishes a strong picture cue.

At the end of each book, we have included three words lists. Can your young learners find all the words in each book with the title letter in them?

Let's learn about the letter **z.**

The letter **Z** can look like this: **Z.**

The letter **Z** can also look like this: **z.**

The letter **z** can be at the beginning of a word, like zebra.

zebra

The letter **z** can be in the middle of a word, like grizzly bear.

gri**zz**ly bear

The letter **z** can be at the

end of a word, like quiz.

qui**z**

Zlata is my best friend. I love to

spend time with **Z**lata. We do many

zany things together.

Zlata and I go to the **z**oo. Her favorite

zoo animal is the **z**ebra. Her striped

shirt makes **Z**lata look like a **z**ebra.

Zlata and I go ice skating. We zigzag

across the frozen ice. **Z**lata zooms by

me on the ice.

Zlata and I like to work on puzzles.

Zlata can gaze at the puzzle for a long

time. **Z**lata loves to work on puzzles.

Zlata and I play with my dog **Z**ap.

Zlata likes to rub **Z**ap's fuzzy fur.

Sometimes **Z**ap's fur makes **Z**lata sneeze!

Zlata and I play quiz games.

Zlata knows most of the answers to

the quiz questions. **Z**lata has an

amazing memory.

I do many things with **Z**lata. Sometimes

we are lazy. Sometimes we are crazy.

It is great to have a friend like **Z**lata.

Fun Facts

A **z**ebra looks like a horse with black and white stripes. **Z**ebras live in herds in southern and eastern Africa. A **z**ebra herd can be made up of several hundred **z**ebras or just a few individuals. Herds help protect **z**ebras from their enemies, which include lions, cheetahs, and leopards. Amazingly, a **z**ebra's stripes, like your fingerprints, are unique. No one **z**ebra has exactly the same stripes as another **z**ebra! A **z**ebra's stripes may help identify it to other members of its herd.

Have you ever been to the **z**oo? How many animals did you see there? A **z**oo is a place where wild animals are kept so that they can be seen and studied. Some **z**oos have animals from all over the world. Other **z**oos choose to keep only one kind of animal, or animals from only one part of the world. An aquarium, for example, is a **z**oo that keeps only fish and aquatic mammals—mammals that live in water. Many **z**oos especially try to help endangered animals.

To Read More

About the Letter Z
Flanagan, Alice K. *Zigzag: The Sound of Z*. Chanhassen, Minn.: The Child's
World, 2000.

About Zebras
Fontes, Justine, and Ron Fontes. *How the Zebra Got Its Stripes*. New York: Golden
Books Family Entertainment, 2002.
Macken, JoAnn Early. *Zebras*. Milwaukee: Weekly Reader Early Learning, 2002.
Markert, Jenny. *Zebras*. Chanhassen, Minn.: The Child's World, 2001.
Reitano, John, and William Haines (illustrator). *What If the Zebras Lost Their
Stripes?*. New York: Paulist Press, 1998.

About Zoos
Mayer, Mercer. *My Trip to the Zoo*. Columbus, Ohio: McGraw Hill, 2002.
Moses, Amy. *At the Zoo*. Chanhassen, Minn.: The Child's World, 1998.
Parr, Todd. *Zoo Do's and Don'ts*. Boston: Little, Brown, 2000.

Words with Z

Words with Z at the Beginning

zany
Zap
Zap's
zebra
zigzag
Zlata
zoo
zooms

Words with Z in the Middle

amazing
crazy
frozen
fuzzy
gaze
grizzly
lazy
puzzle
puzzles
sneeze
zigzag

Words with Z at the End

quiz

About the Authors

Cynthia Klingel has worked as a high school English teacher and an elementary teacher. She is currently the curriculum director for a Minnesota school district. Cynthia Klingel lives with her family in Mankato, Minnesota.

Robert B. Noyed started his career as a newspaper reporter. Since then, he has worked in communications and public relations for a Minnesota school district for more than fourteen years. Robert B. Noyed lives with his family in Brooklyn Center, Minnesota.